This book is for your
beautiful
heart.

words
and your
heart

Kate Jane Neal

FEIWEL AND FRIENDS
NEW YORK

This book is about your heart.

(The little bit inside of you that makes you, you!)

Will you listen very carefully?

Because it's REALLY...

And it might help you
be a happier you

and the people around you
be a happier them!

You see, the words that go into your ears . . .

can actually affect your heart!

(The little bit inside of you that makes you, you!)

Your  can do . . .

AMAZing things!

They can describe things—if they are

BIG.

Or if they are

little.

They can explain stuff,
so you understand that it goes

or spin, tinkle, PING!!!

Words can make you happy . . .

and make you want to sing!

Larrrrrrrrrr

But sometimes words can make us cry.

(We all know what sort of words those are.)

You see, sometimes words can
be like a deadly arrow . . .

that can pierce someone's heart.

(The little bit inside of them that makes them, them!)

Some words can really hurt.

Words have

DUN DUN DARrr

Your words can actually change the
way someone's heart feels.

(The little bit inside of them that makes them, them!)

If someone feels sad,

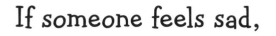

your words can
cheer them up!

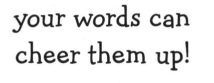

If someone feels weak,
your words can help them feel stronger.

If someone wants to give up,

your words can help them keep going.

Your words can make them giggle,

make them grin,

make them laugh out loud and roll around!

Do you get it?

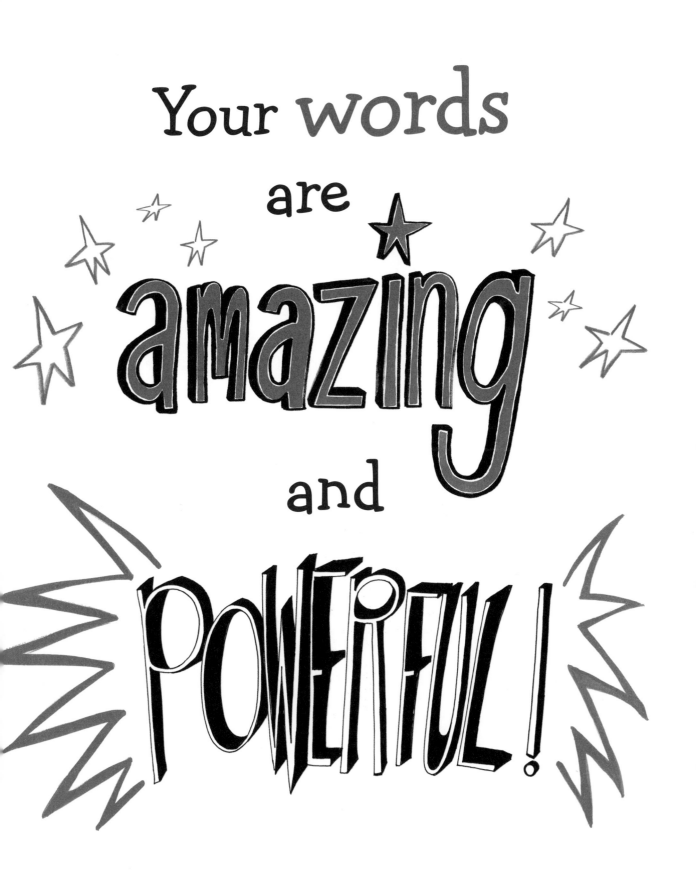

How about we use our words
to look after each other's hearts?

(The little bit inside of us that makes us, us.)

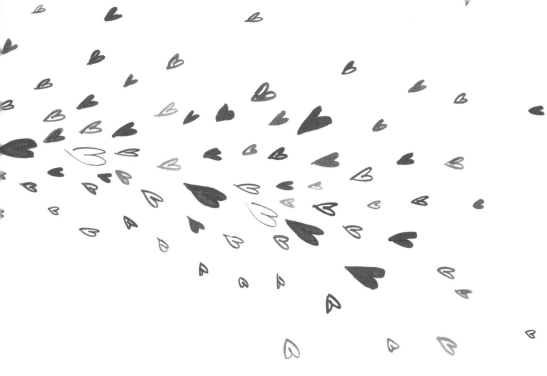

Let's try it together and
see the difference it makes.

Today, somebody's world
can be a better place
because of you!

Thank You!

(Doesn't that make your heart feel good?)

For Thea, Toby, Isaac & Summer x.

A Feiwel and Friends Book

An imprint of Macmillan Publishing Group, LLC

175 Fifth Avenue, New York, NY 10010

Printed in China by RR Donnelley Asia Printing Solutions Ltd., Dongguan City, Guangdong Province.

Our books may be purchased in bulk for promotional, educational, or business use.

Please contact your local bookseller or the Macmillan Corporate and Premium Sales Department at

(800) 221-7945 ext. 5442 or by e-mail at MacmillanSpecialMarkets@macmillan.com.

Library of Congress Cataloging-in-Publication Data is available.

ISBN 978-1-250-16872-6 (hardcover)

Book design by Kate Jane Neal and Kathleen Breitenfeld

Feiwel and Friends logo designed by Filomena Tuosto

Originally published in the UK in 2015 by Wild Goose-Media Ltd.

First US edition, 2017

1 3 5 7 9 10 8 6 4 2

mackids.com